The Pier

By

John Messingham

Cover design by: John Messingham

This book is dedicated to Dad.

One

The beach safety crew had been out and about for an hour in their six-wheeled beach buggy, just making sure everything along the seafront was OK after the tide had gone out. In the background, the sound of a tractor could be heard, making its way up and down the beach, cleaning the sand to remove bottles, glasses and other items left by the previous night's revellers and preparing it for the new day's visitors and activities.

As the beach buggy drew up near the pier, the driver froze for a moment and then, in a startled voice said,

"What's going on here?"

The passenger of the buggy had to turn around towards the front of the buggy as he had been looking around the beach, looking for any large items to pick up. They were now both frozen in their seats and looking forward.

In front of them was the lifeless body of what appeared to be a young woman hanging from the underside of the pier.

As they both sat there trying to make sense of what they had found, a voice comes from the buggy driver's radio.

"What's going on down there? You guys on a tea break already?"

The sound of the voice coming from the radio startled the driver, and she grabbed the radio attached to her jacket.

"You'd better call the police, someone's hung themselves under the pier."

The voice coming from the other end of the radio conversation replied.

"Are you sure? It's not just one of those party blow-up doll things like last time, is it?"

To which the buggy driver replied.

"No. It's a real one this time."

"OK, I'll call the police and tell them what you've got."

While they waited for the police to arrive, the buggy crew, who had now been joined by the tractor driver, thought about how they could keep people away from under the pier until the police arrived and took control of the situation.

Two

DS Becca Brierton was in the reception area of Grimsby's police station in Victoria Street. She had just arrived at the station and was about to make her way to the canteen area to meet up with her new boss, DCI Garner when she heard the deep voice of one of the station's sergeants calling her.

"DS Brierton."

Brierton turned towards the area of the reception where the voice had come from and replied.

"Yes, Sarge. Can I help you with something?"

"We have had a report of a body hanging under the Pier. We are sending officers down there, but they will need someone to take charge of the scene. Can you attend and help, please?"

"Sounds like a uniformed job to me," Brierton replied cheekily.

"But you know I am always willing to help where possible." She continued.

Brierton had joined the Criminal Investigation Department in Hull a few years ago after working as a uniformed officer in the Grimsby area for a few years and had recently been promoted to the rank of Sergeant but had spent her time in uniform serving under the very Sergeant, who was now asking for her help.

"OK, thanks. If you want a lift, some cars are leaving now." The sergeant came back with.

Brierton turned towards the door of the station, saying.

"OK, I will head out now. Will, you get a message to DCI Garner and let him know I have gone down there? He's in the canteen waiting for me."

"Will do." Said the desk sergeant.

She headed out of the station's door and walked towards the parking area. Two police cars passed her with their lights flashing and sirens sounding. A third car pulled up beside her and the officer driving the car lowered the window and called out to her.

"Are you heading down to the Pier? Would you like a lift?"

Brierton turned towards the car and said.

"Go on then. There's no point taking more cars than necessary,"

Brierton hurried towards the car and got into the rear. As she did, the driver pulled away quickly and pressed a couple of buttons on the dashboard of the car that turned on the car's siren and flashing lights.

As the driver drove the car away from the police station. He said, "Well done on your promotion Becca, or do we have to call you Detective Sergeant now?"

Brierton replied. "Thanks, no need to be

so formal, Sarge will do just fine." To which the officer in the front passenger seat replied, sarcastically, "Yeah, won't be long until you take over the station commander's job. Then we'll have to call you ma'am."

Three

 The police car that Brierton was in had made its way through town and was now parked up near the pier alongside the other two police cars that had passed her a few moments before.

Brierton got out of the car and walked towards a concrete ramp to the left of the pier entrance, which led down to the beach area and the underside of the pier.

There was already a large crowd gathered at the top of the ramp, and Brierton had to push her way through so she could get down to the beach. A member of the crowd asked her what was going on, but she made no reply to this request and carried on her way through the crowd. She had always thought that making any comments when you did not understand what had happened would just lead to rumours, and that could make things harder for any relatives or friends of the deceased.

When Brierton and her fellow officers arrived at the bottom of the ramp. She realised they had no cordon in place to keep people off the beach and away from the pier.

"Let's get some tape across the top of the ramp."

One of the officers standing near her quickly responded.

"OK, I have some in the car. I'll go back and get some now."

The officer went back to his car and got some police tape out of the boot. He then returned to the ramp and tied the tape to the building on the side of the ramp and then made his way across the ramp to the other side, where he could tie the tape to another building. As he did this, another officer moved the crowd back out of his way.

Once he had finished tying the tape to the second building, the officer took up a position on the beach side of the tape.

Now that they had secured the area around the scene, all that everyone had to do now was wait for the crime scene manager to arrive. Then the body could be cut down from the underside of the pier and taken to the local mortuary.

Four

Brierton was standing on the beach near the pier talking with another officer when she heard.

"Right then, what do we have today?"

Brierton turned towards the ramp on hearing this and saw Rachel Howton. Howton was a local Crime Scene Manager and had come through the crowd and cordon and was making her way towards the underside area of the pier. And as usual, she had her two-wheeled trolley with her that had large plastic storage boxes tied to it. These boxes contained most of the tools she needed to examine a crime scene and various bags and containers to place any evidence she found at the scene into.

Brierton called out to Howton. "Over here,

Rachel."

Although Brierton knew Rachel Howton well enough to call her by her first name, which was quite informal, she knew Howton would be extremely professional in her role of looking at the scene to determine what had happened. She also knew she was about to get an earful because there had been no photographs taken of the area yet.

"Has the area been photographed?" bellowed Howton as she arrived under the pier.

"Not yet." Replied Brierton, with a slight cringe in her voice.

"We were waiting for you to have a look before we got too close to the body."

As Howton passed Brierton, she muttered under her breath.

"Oh, for goodness' sake. I'll do it."

"It's not as if I have nothing to do all day."

Howton then walked around the area under the Pier and photographed the hanging body from various angles.

Once she had finished taking the photographs, she spent some time looking around where the body was but could see nothing on the ground.

Once she had done this, she called out to Brierton.

"There's nothing here, so can you get some of those uniformed chaps to grab the ladder from the top of my van and get this lady down."

No sooner had she said this than Brierton told one of the uniformed officers to go to Howton's van and get the ladder from it and then told another two officers to make their way under the Pier to assist in getting the body down.

Once the ladder had been extended and placed against a metal beam near the body, one officer went up the ladder.

Two police officers took hold of the body while a third cut the rope halfway between the body and where it was tied to a metal rod under the pier. This would allow the metal bar with the rope tied to it to be removed later and examined if need be.

Once the body had been lowered onto the sand, Howton moved closer to make an initial examination of it. While Howton was examining the body, she called Brierton over and said,

"Can you see that bruising around the women's wrists and ankles?"

Brierton replied, "Yes."

Howton then said, "Those bruises suggest that this woman was tied up before dying, which means we are looking at a murder rather than a suicide. So, you'd better call the station and let them know."

Brierton said. "OK, I will do that now. I will also pass on a description of the body so they can start looking into who it may be."

Brierton took out her phone and called the station to report that it looked like they had a murder on their hands rather than a suicide.

Five

DCI Bob Garner was sitting in Grimsby's police station canteen, having a cup of tea, and waiting to meet up with the new Detective Sergeant that had been assigned to him to gain some experience in her new position.

Garner was now in his thirtieth year as a police officer and had spent most of it in the Humberside area. Apart from a five-year secondment to the Serious Crime Squad in London, where he had helped break up some of the most serious crime gangs in the United Kingdom and put many of their members behind bars.

Having heard sirens leaving the station area and the fact that his new DS had not arrived as expected, he decided to head down to the reception area of the station and see what was going on.

As he got to the reception area, his mobile phone rang in his jacket pocket, so he paused and brought his mobile out of his pocket and answered it.

"DCI Garner."

The person on the other end started to speak, and Garner soon realised he was talking to Cathy Jones, who was the station commander and his direct boss.

"Not sure if you know, but a body was found hanging under the pier this morning."

Cathy continued.

"I hadn't heard that but realised something was going on." Replied Garner.

"Well, it looks like murder rather than a suicide, so can you get down there and take charge?"

"OK, will do, ma'am. I'll report back later and let you know what's going on."

He ended the call and as he did so the Sergeant at the reception desk said,

"Are you heading down to the Pier, sir?"

Garner replied, "Yes."

The Sergeant replied, "OK, DS Brierton has already gone down there to help out."

Garner nodded, said "OK, thanks." and headed for the exit of the reception area and lowered his phone and put it in his pocket as he left the building. He did not have far to walk before he got to his car, which he used to make his way down to the Pier area.

Six

Garner had now made his way down to the seafront and made his way through the crowd and down the ramp and was approaching the area under the pier where Brierton and Howton were waiting for him.

Two other officers were now talking to the council staff and taking notes about what they had initially found.

Garner greeted Brierton and Howton.

"Morning."

To which he received.

"Morning, Sir." From Brierton and a "Morning." From Howton.

"Right, what have you got for me this

morning?"

Brierton started by saying.

"A call came through earlier this morning from the council crew clearing up the beach saying they had found a body hanging under the pier."

"We got here as soon as we could and sealed off the area to keep the public away."

"It wasn't until the body was brought down, then examined, that it became apparent that it was a murder case. Rachel realised the woman must have been dead before being hung here, otherwise, she would have been found before this morning as the beach area would have been busy the previous evening and the level of Rigour Mortis suggests death took place early the previous evening."

Garner replied.

"OK, I guess that any footprints would have been washed away with the morning's tide."

"I looked around and Rachel took some photographs of the area and some of the body hanging, but you're right. There was nothing or any markings around the area of the body." Brierton replied.

Garner paused for a moment and then said.

"Well done, I am glad you were here as the other lot would have just steamed in and got the body down without the slightest consideration of recording the scene."

Just as Garner said this, Brierton's mobile phone started ringing. She took it out of her pocket and answered it.

The voice at the other end belonged to Alan Parsons. Parsons is a retired Detective Constable himself and had returned to the police force as a civilian support officer and was acting as the intelligence and exhibits officer within the police station, so information collected about ongoing investigations in the local area could be collated.

Brierton walked away from where she was standing so she could speak to Parsons without others overhearing their conversation. When she had finished the call, she returned to where Garner was and said.

"We may have a name for the victim."

"A missing person was reported early this morning by a George Diss who lives just outside of the town. His wife, Nicki Diss, is a social worker and was due home after work last night, but never arrived. Her description seems to match the description of the body found under the pier." She continued.

Garner came back with.

"Let's visit him and if we think it is her, get him to identify the body formally and take it from there." Replied Garner, as they both walked towards Garner's car.

Seven

Garner and Brierton arrived at the house of George Diss, Nicki Diss's husband, who had reported his wife missing earlier in the day. Brierton knocked on the door and they both waited.

As the door opened, Garner said.

"Good morning, Mr Diss?"

"Yes." replied the man who was standing in the opened doorway.

"I'm DCI Garner and this is DS Brierton."

Before Garner could finish what, he was about to say, the man had taken on a shocked look and said.

"Is this about my wife?"

Garner replied quickly to this.

"Can we come in, please?" knowing that the quicker they got the George Diss inside and sitting down, the easier this would be. Especially if it was his wife that had been found under the pier.

George Diss beckoned them in saying, "Sorry, yes, please come in."

Once in the house, all three made their way into the living room, where Garner said.

"You may have heard that a body was found under the pier this morning."

"Unfortunately, the description you gave of your missing wife and what she was wearing suggests it might be her."

Garner paused for a moment to allow George to take in the possibility that his wife may be dead.

"Do you have a recent photograph of your wife here?"

"Yes," replied George.

"Give me a moment and I'll get one for you."

The man walked over to a sideboard and took a framed photograph from a shelf in the unit. He bought the photograph back to where Garner and Brierton were standing and handed it to Garner, who looked at it and showed it to Brierton. As soon as Brierton saw the photograph, she looked at Garner and nodded. Garner accepted this as the sign that the lady in the photograph was the victim as Brierton had already seen her on the beach earlier that day.

Garner turned his attention towards George and said in a gentle voice "I am sorry, but it looks like it was your wife we found this morning." Garner then turned his attention back to Brierton and said in a lowered voice "I'll go and call the coroner's office and get them to arrange a formal identification as soon as possible."

As he said this, George realised what had just happened and sat down on the sofa in the room.

As Garner headed for the door to call the station, Brierton sat down in an armchair near to where George was sitting to comfort him if required.

A few minutes later Garner returned to the room where George Diss and Brierton were sitting.

"I have spoken to the coroner's office, and they say you can go down as soon as you feel ready Mr Diss."

George looked up and replied. "Would it be best to go straight away, I mean, there is still a chance that it isn't Nicki, isn't there?"

Brierton stood up and as she did, she said to George, "You're right, it is probably best to go now."

George responded to this by just nodding and then standing up as well. As all three headed out of the room's door, George picked up a black bomber-style jacket that was hanging on the back of a chair that was to the side of the door.

As they left the house, Garner handed Brierton his car keys and said, "Take my car, I asked for a squad car to pick me up and take me back to the station."

Eight

Brierton and George Diss arrived in the small car park of the coroner's office. Once out of the car they made their way to the rear door of the building, where they were met by a smartly dressed woman.

"Hi, Leigh." Said, Brierton.

"Hello Rebecca" Leigh replied and then turned her attention directly to George Diss and welcomed him by saying.

"Hello Mr Diss, please come in."

Leigh then led them to a small room within the building that was furnished with a sofa, two matching armchairs and a small table in between the sofa and the two chairs.

Once everyone was in the room, Leigh said.

"Please take a seat" and indicated to them both that they should sit down on the sofa on the far side of the coffee table.

"The coroner will be with you soon and explain what will happen next."

"Can I get either of you a drink? Tea, coffee, or water?"

Brierton replied, "no thanks, I'm fine," and turned towards George Diss and asked, "How about you? Would you like a drink?"

"A glass of water would be good," George said.

"OK, I won't be a moment." Said Leigh as she walked towards and exited through the room's door. Closing the door behind her.

Once Leigh had left the room, George turned to Brierton and asked.

"What happens now?"

Brierton replied, "The coroner will come in and see us. He will have a photograph to show you and you just need to tell him if it is your wife or not."

"We all appreciate this will be hard, so please take your time. There is no rush."

The door of the room opened, and a stern-looking man entered. He was carrying a glass of water and had a brown paper folder under his arm.

He closed the door behind himself and asked.

"Who is this for?" in a subdued voice which did not match his demeanour.

George looked up at the man and raised his hand a bit, indicating the drink was for him, at which point the male handed him the glass and said.

"There you go."

He then looked around the room and sat down in one of the armchairs on the opposite side of the table to Brierton and George Diss.

He placed the paper folder on the table in front of him and sat back in the chair.

"I have here a photograph of the female who was found this morning in the area of the pier."

"The police inform me that they believe this person to be your wife."

He paused to allow George to take these statements in for a moment before continuing to say.

"In a moment I will open this folder and let you see the photograph."

"And all I need you to do is tell me if the lady in the photograph is your wife or not. Please understand there is no rush and if you feel the need to take a moment before indicating if it is your wife or not, then please do so."

The coroner paused once again and then opened the folder that he had now moved towards George.

George looked at the photograph for a moment in silence and then burst into tears.

Through his tears, he said.

"Yes, that's her, that's my Nicki."

Once George had composed himself a bit, he asked.

"Can I go home now, please?"

Brierton replied.

"Yes, I'll take you home."

Both got up and left the room to head back to George's house.

Once both had left the room and made their way back to the car which was parked in the coroner's office car park, Brierton opened the car's front passenger door and allowed George to get into the car.

As Brierton started to close the car door, she lent down a bit towards him and said.

"Can you give me a moment to call my boss and let him know we are heading back to your house?"

Brierton took her mobile phone out of her

pocket and called Garner.

"Hello, Sir."

"George Diss has just confirmed to the coroner that it is his wife, Nicki Diss."

The voice on the other end of the call said.

"OK, take him home and wait for a family liaison to arrive. I will call them now and get them to assign someone as soon as possible. Once they arrive, head down to the social services office and see if you can get some information on any cases she was involved with. In case there is a link with what has happened to her."

To which Brierton replied. "OK, will do."

Nine

Brierton walked into the local offices of social services and made her way to the reception desk where a young male was sitting.

"Hi, I'm DS Brierton." She announced, holding up a small leather wallet that held her identification card.

"I need to speak to someone about one of your colleagues please, ideally, a manager if possible." She continued.

The young man came back with, "Please take a seat, I will see if I can get someone down to help you," as he picked up the handset of the telephone on his desk.

"Can you come down, please? The police are here."

"OK, I'll tell them you're on your way."

The receptionist put down the handset, looked over towards Brierton and said.

"Someone will be with you in a moment."

"Thanks." Replied Brierton.

Within a few minutes, another male appeared in the reception area and walked towards where Brierton was sitting and said.

"Hello, my name is James Bryde. How can I help?"

"I want to talk to you about Nicki Diss."

"Unfortunately, she was found dead this morning and we want to find out if her death is related to a case she may have been involved with. Either current or in the past."

James took a moment to take what Garner had just said to him in and then replied.

"You mean she was killed?"

"Sorry, but yes, we are treating her death as a murder."

"Is this related to the body found under the Pier this morning? I heard something about it on the radio as I was driving into work."

"I cannot discuss the details but yes, it is."

James led Brierton through the office building to the office where Nicki Diss worked.

As they entered the office, Brierton said.

"Can you think of any cases that may give concern over Nicki's safety?"

James replied.

"Nothing comes to mind. It would take me a few minutes, but I could get a list of the cases she was working on if that would help." He continued.

Brierton responded by saying. "Yes please, that would be great." And as she finished saying this, James suggested that she "Take a seat." And he left the office.

After a short time, James returned to the office clutching a piece of paper.

"I have the case list," He announced as he entered the office. And handed it to Brierton.

"Thanks" She replied.

She started to look through the list and as she did, she asked.

"Do you know what time Nicki left the office yesterday?"

James seemed to ponder for a moment about the question he had just been asked and then said. "I think she left shortly before me at about five fifteen."

"Do you know if she would have been heading straight home or going somewhere else first?"

"I couldn't say to be honest."

"OK, thanks for that, and thanks again for the case list. I'll get back to you if I have any further questions, you may be able to answer." And then made her way out of the office and back to her car so she could return to the station.

Ten

Once Brierton had returned to the office, she sat down at her desk and looked through the case list she had been given at the social services office. Nicki Diss had only been a social worker for about two years, so she was not the most experienced member of the local social work team. All the cases on the list were related to care services for elderly residents in the area.

As nothing on the list gave Brierton any immediate concern, she put the list to one side and turned her attention towards DCI Garner who was sitting at his desk reading through his notes and a copy of the missing person's report relating to Nicki Diss that had now been given to him.

He looked up at Brierton and said.

"One thing that puzzles me is why did the husband wait until this morning to call in about his wife not coming home. Did he know she was missing?"

"Most people call the police within a couple of hours of someone appearing to go missing."

"I wonder if the fact George Diss waited until this morning has some sort of meaning and if this would be relevant to the case."

Garner looked towards Allan Parsons who was sitting at the other end of the office.

"Allan, it's getting late now but, in the morning, can you see if you can get hold of the phone records for both Nicki and George Diss for the last week or so and see if it sheds some light on this."

Parsons replied. "OK, I'll get on to that first thing in the morning."

Brierton also called over to Allan Parsons.

"Allan, can you file this list into the evidence files before you leave in case we need it later, please?"

At this, Parsons got up from his desk and made his way towards Brierton. Once at her desk, he took the list from her and made his way back to his desk.

Garner and Brierton left for the evening, followed by Parsons once he had filed the case list into the evidence box, he had prepared.

Eleven

The next morning, Parsons was composing the email which would start the process of getting Nicki and George Diss's telephone records, the door of the office opened, and a female uniformed officer rushed into the office and headed straight to where Garner was sitting.

"Sir," she said excitedly.

"We carried out some door-to-door enquiries yesterday around the area of the social services offices and the Pier, and I have just received a statement taken from a barman in one of the bars in the marketplace near to the pier."

The officer caught her breath and then continued.

"He said that George Diss and another

man had a big row in the bar where he was working."

She paused again as she was having trouble controlling her breath, as she knew this information could be a big turning point in the investigation. Once she had caught her breath again, she continued.

"The barman said that the man threatened to have a good time with Diss's wife if he didn't repay the money he owed to his boss within the next few days."

"The barman said although he had seen the other man in the pub before, he doesn't know who he is, but he was very aggressive and had a look of someone who would back up his statements. Even if it meant being violent."

Once the officer had finished speaking, Garner said.

"That's good work, thanks for that." then looked at Brierton and said.

"Get onto family liaison and see if George Diss is still at his house? I think we need to speak to him as soon as possible about this row."

Brierton picked up her mobile telephone that was on her desk and called the officer that had been assigned to look after George Diss and had a brief conversation with them. She then came back to Garner. "He is still at home and Nicki Diss's mother Lesley is there with him."

"OK, let's head down there," Garner said as he stood up and headed for the office door followed closely behind by Brierton.

As he made his way out of the office, Garner turned back towards the officer that had given him the details of the argument and said.

"Can you look into if there are any CCTV images of this argument in the pub and look to see if you can track down anything from the surrounding area that may help with anything that happened afterwards."

Garner and Brierton left the office and made their way to the car park where they got into Brierton's car and headed back to the Diss's house.

Twelve

George Diss was in his kitchen talking to Nicki's mother, Lesley Garth, and the family liaison officer when there was a loud knock on the front door. The knock did not surprise any of them as Brierton had spoken to the liaison officer who was with Diss and told them she and Garner were coming to the house. The officer had told the others of the expected visitors.

As the officer got up from their chair, Diss asked.

"Do you think they will have more of an idea of what happened to Nicki?"

The officer replied, "I'm not sure."

The officer then headed to the door to let Garner and Brierton in.

As Garner entered the kitchen he said "Hello." to Diss and continued with, "We need to speak to you about an argument you had with someone in a pub the other day."

Diss got up from his chair and walked over to the window of the room and replied.

"That was Mick Kurzwell. Do you think he had something to do with this?"

Once Diss had finished speaking, Brierton looked at Garner and said, "I know Kurzwell. He's a nasty piece of work."

Garner looked at Diss and said. "How much do you owe?"

Diss continued with "Oh, you know what he deals with in the area."

Garner replied. "Yeah, I know all about him."

Diss then carried on by saying, "Just over ten grand. I got into debt with his boss over some bets that didn't work out so well for me. The trouble is he adds interest every day and eventually Mick appears on the scene if you don't keep up with the payments. It's my fault for getting into this situation."

Lesley started to speak and in a choked voice said.

"Nicki had spoken to me about this Kurzwell guy. She said he was hanging around outside her office once and when she came out of work, he approached her. He told her that if George didn't pay off the money, he owed. She may need to come to some sort of arrangement with him to keep the interest at a minimum."

Garner had decided by this point that they would need to speak to Kurzwell to see if he was involved in the killing of Nicki. Although he knew Kurzwell had a history of violence and intimidation. Killing someone because their husband owed money seemed a bit beyond his previous activities, but then again, there was always a chance he had progressed in his violence and that he was their man. Garner was also considering looking into Diss more just in case there was an insurance angle.

"OK, we're going to speak to Kurzwell," Garner announced. "Thank you both for your help."

 He finished speaking, turned and made his way back towards the front door and out of the house. As he left, he took out his phone so he could call Allan Parsons back at the station. As he now had the name of the man Diss had argued with while in the pub, he could set about finding him and questioning him further. He knew it might take some time to locate Kurzwell, as Garner knew he moved about a lot to make it harder for the police to monitor him.

"Hello Allan, this is Garner. I need to locate Mick Kurzwell. It looks like he was the one who was arguing with George Diss, and may have made some threats towards Nicki Diss."

"Can you look into the current intelligence we have on Kurzwell and get back to me with any locations where we may find him."

Garner paused while Allan replied and then responded, "OK, thanks, I'll wait for your call." And ended the call.

Thirteen

Mick Kurzwell was sitting in his office within an arcade near the entrance to the Pier. He was counting cash he had collected from his network of street dealers the night before.

Kurzwell had moved to the area two years ago and took up the role of an enforcer for a local crime family after his predecessor had been killed. Once he had established himself in the area, he took control of the local drug-dealing operations and quickly eliminated most of the other suppliers by either threatening them or, if the rumours were true, having some of them killed.

Outside the arcade, two police cars pulled up. Officers had got out of the cars and while some of them entered the arcade, a couple of them had made their way around the back of the arcade where there was another exit door that led out onto the beach.

Once all the officers had taken up their positions, Garner and Brierton approached the door to the office. Brierton knocked on the door and stepped back. With Kurzwell's history of violence, none of the officers knew how this was going to go, although Kurzwell had never shown aggression towards the police in the past his reputation meant that if he was cornered his reaction would be unpredictable.

The door remained closed, so Brierton stepped forward and knocked again. As she did, the radios of the officers inside the arcade all burst into life.

"He made a run for it out the back, but we have got him."

As this message ended, the door to the office opened and one officer that had gone round the back of the arcade appeared.

"We've got him in here." The officer announced and then moved back into the office.

Brierton and Garner followed the officer back into the office and saw that Kurzwell was sitting in a chair near the rear door with his hands handcuffed behind him.

Garner looked around the office and saw the pile of cash on the desk and walked towards it.

"Looks like you had a good day yesterday," Garner said. "But we will come back to that later."

Garner turned towards Kurzwell and said, "We want to speak to you about Nicki Diss."

"Who's Nicki Diss? What about her?" Kurzwell replied.

Garner moved towards Kurzwell "So, you don't know who Nicki Diss is but you know it's a female. Well, she was found dead under the Pier this morning. Just outside this office and we know about the threats you made towards her in the social services office car park and while you were arguing with her husband recently. So, you are coming with us for a chat at the station."

Garner looked towards the officer standing beside Kurzwell and said, "Take him to the station and lock him up. Once we have searched this office, we will come and interview him." Then, turning towards Brierton continued by saying, "Let's have a good look around as I am sure there will be plenty of interesting stuff tucked away in here."

Kurzwell was helped to his feet by the officer, and, looking at Garner, said. "You'll find nothing here cos I had nothing to do with anyone's death."

Brierton replied, "Find nothing, that's the best one I have heard all day. So far, and I doubt there will be better."

Kurzwell just glared at Brierton and then turned to Garner and said, "I suppose you'll want to talk about the usual subject as well while I'm visiting your place."

As Kurzwell said this he was led out of the office and through the arcade to where the cars were parked outside.

Fourteen

Once Kurzwell had been taken out of the office and on his way to the police station. Garner, Brierton, and two of the officers that had arrived with them started to search the office.

One of the uniformed officers said, "Are we looking for anything in particular, sir?"

Garner replied, "There is a possibility he is linked with the body found under the pier. Which is why we wanted to speak to him, but his reaction suggests he thought we were here for another reason, so collect and bag up anything you think is related to his usual businesses?"

The officer replied, "OK, sir," and carried on looking around the office for anything that seemed out of place for an amusement arcade office.

Brierton made her way over to where Garner was standing and said, "What did Kurzwell mean when he said about talking about the usual subject?"

Garner said, "It relates to my time in London. I was part of a team that spent years looking into a crime family operating in London and eventually got the evidence together to break up the family gang and put most of them behind bars. Kurzwell worked for the family as a thug, much like he does around here."

Brierton said, "Oh I see, I knew he had a history down in London but never had any dealings with him in the past because I was on the other side of the river in Hull when he came to the area."

Garner said, "You're the lucky one there. I knew him here years ago before I went to London. He appeared on the scene down there just after me. It's like he was following me like a bad penny. And when I came back up here, he once again appeared on the scene."

"So, what is the usual subject between you?" Brierton asked again.

To which Garner replied, "When we arrested the London crime family members, we also arrested Kurzwell but he must have done some sort of deal with the prosecutors because for all his antics while working for the family, which I am sure included murder he spent very little time in prison. Since then, the couple of times I have interviewed him about his activities here, he has never let on what happened. The thing is, I'm sure he knows a lot more than we ever got out of him about the crime family and that information could help put a lot more people behind bars."

"I see," said Brierton, "Will you bring that up when we talk to him later today?"

To which Garner replied, "Probably not, we will just concentrate on finding out what happened to Nicki for now. I am sure I will get more chances to talk to him about other things in the future. Let's face it, he will be back with us again in the future"

Brierton nodded in agreement and returned to the matter in hand of searching the office.

After about thirty minutes of searching, there was quite a pile of evidence bags containing cash and mobile telephones on the floor in the centre of the office. Both were good indications of Kurzwell's drug activities and surprised neither Garner nor Brierton.

As the search continued, Garner's phone rang so he took his phone out and answered it. He listens to the caller for a moment and then says "OK, we will be right over." And hung up the phone.

Garner turned to Brierton and says. "That was Rachel Howton. She has the autopsy report and wants us to go over and go through it with her."

"You guys carry on searching here and then go back to the station with everything you have bagged up."

"OK, Sir," one of the officers responds.

Garner and Brierton left the arcade office leaving the uniformed officers to carry on with the search on their own.

Fifteen

Rachel Howton was at her desk in the office at the back of her Pathology laboratory and as Garner and Brierton walked in she said.

"Hello, you two."

Garner responded, "Hello, what do you have for us?"

Rachel Howton picked up some papers from her desk and looked at them as she started to speak.

"I have the initial autopsy report for Nicki Diss. The estimated time of death is between 6 and 8 pm the night before she was found under the pier."

Garner responded, "That means she was probably killed somewhere else then as there is no way somebody could be left hanging under the pier that long and nobody finding her before first light,"

Garner looked over towards Brierton and carried on with "What do you think?"

Brierton responded "True, there are too many people walking along the beach during that time of the evening for a body to be missed."

Rachel Howton carried on speaking.

"The bruises I found on the wrists and ankles appear to have been made by a rope of some kind. They are too symmetric to be caused by someone fighting someone else off."

"So, do you know what the actual cause of death was?" Garner asked.

Rachel Howton responded, "Yes, asphyxiation, but again, the bruises around her neck suggest she was hung rather than strangled."

"I've sent samples off for a full toxicology report, but the results will take some time to get back to me. One thing I did find was a needle puncture mark on the side of the neck. It was hidden by the bruising, but I spotted it."

Brierton asked "Just one?"

To which Rachel responded "Yes, it's located on the top of her shoulder, which is an odd place for it to be a result of drug use by her and the fact there is only one is unusual for a drug user. I would think it was the result of someone injecting her with something to subdue her."

Garner paused for a moment, taking in all that he had just been told and then said.

"Brilliant work Rachel, as usual. We need to get back to the office then and see if Allan has got anything from the CCTV cameras around the pier area the night before Nicki was found."

With this new information, DCI Garner and DS Brierton left the office and headed back to their own office.

Sixteen

Garner walked into the murder team's office where Allan Parson was sitting at his desk watching CCTV footage.

Allan Parsons said "Is DS Brierton with you? All the stuff from Kurzwell's office search has been taken to the main evidence store as there was far too much to be stored here."

Garner came back with.

"Yes, we got the message you had left at the reception, so she has gone straight down to look through it to see if there is anything related to the death of Nicki Diss."

Garner continued.

"We have just got back from seeing

Rachel Howton and she says there was a needle mark on Nicki Diss's shoulder. Do you recall anything that would indicate that Nicki used drugs?"

"No, nothing," Parsons said.

Garner carried on by saying "OK, do some cross-referencing and see if you can find any other links between Nicki and Kurzwell other than the link we now know about with her husband."

Parsons replied, "OK, it will take some time, but I will see what I can find."

As Parsons turned his attention back to his computer DS Brierton walked back into the office holding an evidence bag and said.

"Sir, this syringe and liquid were found in Kurzwell's office by the officers."

Garner looked at the evidence bag and said.

"Great, get that sent over to Rachel so she can analyse the contents to see if they match anything found in Nicki's blood."

As Brierton left the room, Garner walked over to Parsons and said.

"Have you had any luck with the CCTV footage from the Pier and surrounding area?"

"Not yet," Parsons responded. "I'm working backwards but it is taking some time."

Garner started to head for the office door.

"OK, I'm going to get a cup of tea. Do you want one?" Garner asks.

Parsons replied "Thanks, a coffee would be great. Better make it a large one."

Seventeen

Garner was standing in the corridor where the interview rooms are when Brierton joined him.

"I've sent the syringe and liquid over to Rachel Howton's office, but she says it will take some time to get the results of what it is back to us," Brierton said, "But I took a photo of them in case that is useful in the interview. She continues.

Garner replied, "That's great, let's get this interview started." As he opened the door and went into the interview room.

Mick Kurzwell and his solicitor were sitting quietly at a small table in the interview room. Garner and Brierton entered the room and sat down in the two seats on the opposite side of the table.

Garner indicated to Brierton to start the interview by turning on the recorder mounted on the wall near the end of the table. Once she had started the recording device, she announced.

"This interview is being carried out by myself, Detective Sergeant Brierton and Detective Chief Inspector Garner."

"Also present are Mick Kurzwell and his legal representative."

Garner then took the lead in the interview process by asking.

"What was your relationship with Nicki and George Diss?"

Kurzwell simply replied.

"No comment."

Brierton then interjected.

"Can you tell us about the threats you made towards George Diss and his wife in the pub?"

Kurzwell replied with the same.

"No comment." Reply as last time.

Brierton carried on.

"We understand George Diss owes you a lot of money, well he owes your boss the money. Were you acting on instructions from him, or did you kill Nicki because George Diss not paying up made you look bad at your job?"

This line seemed to have the desired effect on Kurzwell. He became visibly angered by what was being said and exploded into a rage.

"I didn't kill anyone."

Garner waited for Kurzwell to calm down and then asked.

"Are you able to account for your movements over the last week?"

To which Kurzwell replied angrily.

"Are you not listening to me? I had nothing to do with her death, so I don't need to prove anything to you about what I have been doing."

Once again Garner waited for Kurzwell to finish his ranting and pushed the photo of the syringe and liquid towards Kurzwell saying.

"We found this in your office and while we don't know what the liquid is yet. But I expect it will match what was used to subdue Nicki Diss so you could kill her."

Kurzwell seemed to hit boiling point at this point and shouted at Garner. "No, I had nothing to do with her death."

Realising Kurzwell was too wound up now to be interviewed with any success Garner decided to pause the interview and let him calm down a bit.

"OK, you can stay here and discuss this with your solicitor and let us know when you're ready to co-operate."

At this, Brierton announces that the interview is being suspended and both she and Garner leave the interview room and head back to their office.

Eighteen

As Garner and Brierton entered their office they nearly tripped over Parsons who was rushing out of the office.

He said, "I was just coming down to the interview room to get you. We have some CCTV footage taken during the night Nicki Diss was hung under the pier."

Garner replied "Great, I'm guessing the way you were heading out tells us there is something useful in the video."

Parsons replied, "Yes, it shows someone carrying someone else towards the underside of the pier. Although we cannot see who it is as they have their face covered, we can see clearly what car they were driving."

Garner said, "OK, let's have a look."

Garner and Parsons made their way to Parson's desk where he sat down and grabbed his computer mouse. He clicked on the screen and the CCTV footage started to play.

As they watched they saw a car pull up near the slipway that went down towards the area under the pier, and someone get out of the driver's seat. They moved to and opened the rear door nearest the slipway and pulled what appeared to be a body out of the rear seat. They then carried the body down the slipway and out of view from the camera.

Parsons said, "No cameras cover the underside of the pier so we cannot see what goes on there."

Garner replied, "Never mind this is a real step forward. Do we know whose car that is?"

Parsons turned around, looked at Garner and said.

"Yes, we do. It belongs to George Diss."

"Do we know where the car is now?" Garner said.

"Yes, as soon as I realised whose car it was, I got the control room to send a couple of cars down to Diss's house and see if the car was there. It is parked around the corner from the house, so they are watching the car and house to secure any evidence and are waiting for you to decide the next move."

"Right, get hold of Rachel Howton and get her down to George Diss's house and check the car out."

"We need to bring Diss in for an interview. I think this information gives us enough for an arrest." Garner said.

Brierton looked at him and said, "I agree, shall we get uniform to bring him in?"

"No, let's go down and get him ourselves," Garner replied.

Garner and Brierton left the office and headed down to George Diss's house.

As they did Garner looked back towards Parsons and said.

"Tell the officers down there that if Diss leaves the house then arrest him."

Nineteen

Garner and Brierton arrived at George Diss's house, and once they had got to the front door, Garner knocked on it. A short time passed, and George Diss opened the door.

"Hello, Mr Diss. Can we come in, please?" Garner said.

"Sure, come on in," Diss replied as he moved aside to allow Garner to enter the house.

Once Garner had passed Diss and was standing in the hallway of the house he turned towards Diss and said.

"We have viewed some CCTV video footage from the night that your wife was killed."

"The video shows someone using your car to take your wife's body to the pier, so I am arresting you on suspicion of your wife's murder."

As Garner explained his rights to Diss, Brierton who had remained between Diss, and the door said.

"Please put your arms behind your back." And as she said this, Diss complied, but looked around at her and said, "I have done nothing wrong. Why are you doing this to me?"

As he protested, Brierton grabbed for her handcuffs and placed them on his wrists. She then took hold of his arm and led him out of the house, followed by Garner. All three made their way along the garden path and through the gate at the end of it. Once outside the garden, Garner opened the closest rear car door to them. Garner helped Diss into the back of the car and then shut the door. Brierton was now getting into the back of the car to sit beside Diss while they drove back to the station.

As Garner was getting into the car, he beckoned one of the officers sitting in the police car across the road from the house to come over to him.

As the officer got nearer to Garner's car, Garner said. "Seal of the house, front and back and treat it as a possible crime scene and tell the officers round the corner to tell Rachel Howton to search the car they are watching."

The officer replied, "OK sir, will do."

Garner then closed his car door and drove back to the station. Once back at the station Garner got out of the car and opened the door where Diss was sitting. He helped Diss out of the car and once he was out Brierton got out of the car behind him. They lead Diss into the station and along a corridor to the custody suite. Once they were standing in front of the custody desk, Garner explained that Diss had been arrested on suspicion of murdering his wife and he wanted him remanded in police custody while they made further enquiries. The custody sergeant went through the formalities and then said to an officer standing in the custody suite.

"Take Mr Diss through to the interview room one."

The officer complied with this order and headed to the interview room area of the custody suite followed by Garner and Brierton.

Twenty

The white van of Rachel Howton arrived at the location where George Diss's car was parked and as she approached the car, pulling her trolley of plastic boxes behind her, one officer standing near it said.

"We picked up the keys for it from the house and unlocked it for you."

Howton replied, "Thanks, it's nice to have someone thinking ahead as it makes my life easier which is always a good idea." To which the officer just laughed.

Howton walked up to the car and tried to open the boot. Her experience told her she should start with the boot area, as this is where abducted people and dead bodies usually ended up. The boot did not open, so she looked back towards the officer who had spoken to her and asked.

"Oh dear, Is there a button on the remote to open the boot? If so, can you press it as the boot is still locked?"

With this, the officer took a small plastic evidence bag containing the key out of his pocket and looked at it and said.

"Yeah, there is, sorry about that."

He then pointed it towards the car and pressed the button to unlock the boot and as he did the boot lid clicked and raised a little.

As Howton lifted the boot lid, she straight away noticed a piece of rope within it. She picked the rope up and examined it more. It looked similar in colour and thickness to the rope used to hang Nicki Diss's body under the pier. Realising this could be a link between the car and Nicki's death, she took a large plastic evidence bag out of one of her plastic boxes and placed the rope into it and sealed the bag closed.

She then looked around the boot area of the car further but apart from the rope, the boot of the car was remarkably empty. She lifted the carpet to reveal the location where the car's spare wheel was and looked around it. Everything seemed to be in its place, all the moulded areas that held various tools for the car appeared to have something within them. So, she replaced the carpet and made her way to the driver's door.

She spent the next hour examining the inside of the car carefully, but apart from the rope in the boot, there didn't seem to be anything out of the ordinary in the car. She knew that once it was recovered back to the crime lab, it could be examined in more detail. Her next move was to get the rope she had found in the boot compared to the rope found at the pier.

She gathered her boxes up and placed them back on her trolley and started to make her way back to her van. As she did she spoke to the officer who had the keys to the car she had just searched.

"Can you arrange for the car to be transported back to the workshop at the station, please? I will have a closer look at it once it is there and send my report to DCI Garner as soon as I can.

Twenty-One

Once inside the interview room, the uniformed officer asked Diss to sit down at the table in the centre of the room. Garner and Brierton had followed them into the room and sat down at the table opposite Diss.

Brierton turned on the recording device on the table and said.

"Present in the room are DS Brierton, DCI Garner and Mr George Diss."

"Can you confirm for the recording that you have been read your rights and that you understand them?"

Diss replied with a nod of his head and a simple "Yes."

Brierton continued.

"Can you also confirm you have refused legal representation for this interview but understand you can change your mind at any point during it?"

Diss again replied.

Yes. I understand but I have nothing to hide or worry about."

DCI Garner then takes over the interview.

"OK, let's get on then."

"Can you tell us when you last saw Nicki and how things were between you?"

Diss paused for a moment and then said.

"I saw her in the morning on the day she went missing. We have been having a few problems but nothing really serious."

Garner responded with, "OK, are there any third parties involved here?"

"No, nothing like that. It's just that both of us work long hours and it left little time to spend together. As a result of this, we have grown apart."

"Why did you not report Nicki missing until the following morning?"

"Sometimes, when things were heated between us, she would stay at Lesley's, you know, her mum. But when I called her mobile in the morning and didn't get an answer. I called her mum. She said Nicki had not stayed with her, which is when I got worried and called you."

"Why did you not call her the evening before she was found?"

"We had a big argument in the morning, and she said she was going to stay with her mum that night. So, I decided to let have some space and calm down."

Just as Garner was going to carry on with his questions, the door to the interview room opened and Allan Parsons walked in.

Brierton looked towards the door to see who had walked in, realising it was Parsons, she said.

"For the recording, Allan Parsons has entered the room."

Parsons headed to where Garner was

sitting and whispered into his ear.

"Sorry to disturb you sir but could you go to your office as there has been a development concerning the case."

Garner looked towards Brierton and nodded to her as he said.

"OK, we will pause the interview for now."

Brierton moved her hand towards the recording device and with her finger hovering in front of the button to stop the recording, she said.

"Interview suspended at Three Fifty-Five PM." And then she pressed the button to stop the recording.

Garner and Brierton stood up and made their way to the interview room door where Parsons was now standing and as they did, George Diss asked.

"What is going on?"

Garner paused and turned round towards Diss and replied.

"I am not sure. But as soon as I know

something I will come back and tell you."

Garner and Brierton left the room leaving Diss and the uniformed officer sitting by the door.

Twenty-Two

As soon as Garner and Brierton were outside the interview room and the door was closed.

Parsons said, "The local social services office called the station front desk and said, Nicki Diss's mother Lesley Garth cannot be contacted. They said that she was going into the office today but never showed up. Due to what had happened to her daughter, one of her colleagues tried to contact her but with no success. A couple of officers had been sent round to her house to see if she was there. When the officers arrived, they found the front door to the house was open. They entered the house and had a look round, but there was no one there. However, there were signs that a struggle had taken place as some of the furniture in the living room had been knocked over."

Garner replied, "Are the officers still there?"

Parsons replied, "Yes, they have been posted to both the front and back doors of the house and are treating it as a crime scene."

Turning his attention to Brierton, Garner said.

"OK, you head down to the house and see what you can make of the situation. I will go back to the interview room and see if Diss can shed any light on this. Then I'll make my way down to the house. Then turning his attention back to Parsons, he said, If you go back to the office and keep trying every number we have for her to see if you can track her down."

Brierton and Parsons both responded with "Will do," then Brierton headed off out of the station and Parsons headed back to the team's office.

Garner turned back towards the interview room door, opened it, and re-entered the room.

George Diss was still sitting at the table in

the room.

Diss looked over to Garner and asked. "What is going on? Is there any news about what happened to Nicki?"

Garner replied. "There is nothing new regarding your wife, but your mother-in-law seems to have gone missing, and no one can contact her. Do you know where she may be or if she had anything planned for today?"

Diss replied in a slightly raised voice, "She had nothing planned that she told me about. You have to remember my relationship with her is not the greatest so she rarely shared much with me."

Garner thought for a moment and then looked at the officer sitting at the back of the interview room and said.

"Right, OK. Can you wait here with Mr Diss, please? We will go and see if we can find out what's going on."

Looking back at Diss, Garner said.

"We will need to carry on with this interview later. So, for now, you will be held here while I go and see what is going on regarding your mother-in-law."

To which Diss replied, "I don't see what else I can tell you. Keeping me here is just a waste of everyone's time."

Garner then made his way out of the interview room and headed out of the station to make his way to Lesley Garth's house.

Twenty-Three

Garner arrived at Lesley Garth's house and made his way to the front door. The door was now manned by a uniformed officer. As Garner approached the door, the officer pushed the door open and said.

"Afternoon sir."

Garner stopped and replied.

"Hi. Do I need to suit up?"

The officer replied.

"No, Sir. Ms Howton was here a while ago but had left now, so you're safe."
Garner smiled at the officer and entered the house.

Inside the house, there was a lot of activity. Various uniformed officers were milling around, searching for anything that could help work out what had happened to Lesley Garth.

While Garner was gathering his thoughts and working out where to head first. A voice called out from the living room.

"Is that you, Sir?"

Garner recognised the voice as that of Brierton.

"I think we have something here in the living room."

Garner followed the voice and made his way into the living room of the house.

"Sir, it looks like we are dealing with an abduction. There are signs of a struggle in this room and this box of files has been emptied."

On the living room table, there was a metal file storage box with the lid open and some of the files scattered across the tabletop.

As Garner walked into the living room, Brierton started to talk again.

"Lesley Garth is also a social worker like her daughter and had been for many years. The files in the box all appear to be very old cases she had worked on."

Garner stood for a moment looking around the room and then turned towards Brierton and said.

"OK, grab the files up so we can take them with us. We'll leave the uniforms here to carry on searching and head down to the office." Garner replied.

Brierton gathered up the files on the table and put them into the case, which she closed and picked up. Both then headed out of the house and back to Garner's car which was parked just along the road from the house.

Twenty-Four

Garner and Brierton arrived back at the police station and made their way through the building back to the office where they worked from. Once they were back in their office, Brierton said.

"I'll get these files stored."

Garner replied.

"OK, I'll start thinking of where we go next on this one. Do you have the missing person report? We will need to work out Lesley's movements before she went missing."

"Yes, I have it here," Brierton replied as she opened the leather folder where she kept paperwork and forms. And passed the missing person report to Garner.

While Garner was reading the report, Brierton went across to the other end of the office where Allan Parsons was sitting.

"Can you place these files into the evidence store please?" Brierton asked.

"OK, will do," Parsons replied. "Do you want me to record the details of each file?"

Brierton thought for a moment and as tempted as she was to allow Parsons to carry out a long-winded exercise in evidence logging. She thought of the case list she had been given earlier and decided to go easy on him.

"Give the social services office a call and ask for James Bryde and see if he can send you a case file list or whatever they call it for Lesley Garth. He was the guy I met with at the offices when I visited yesterday."

He then grabbed another cardboard evidence box from a small pile of boxes next to the shelves and placed the file storage case into it. He then picked up a box lid from a pile of lids next to the boxes and placed it onto the box and then placed the box on his desk ready for when he had the case list, he could store with it and used to enter the file details into the evidence log.

Twenty-Five

Rachel Howton walked into the team's office and said.

"I have the results of the tests that have been carried out on the liquid found in Kurzwell's office, the rope that had been used to hang Nicki Diss's body under the pier and the rope found in the back of George Diss's car."

"I thought I would pop up with it and see how you are getting on with the case and if there was anything else I could help with."

Once she was in the office, she made her way over to Garner's desk and handed the report over to him, saying.

"The liquid did not match anything in Nicki Diss's blood, but I think you should read this."

Garner looked at the piece of paper. It showed that there was nothing found in the car except for the rope, which was the same type of rope that had been used to hang the body of Nicki Diss under the pier. The report also confirmed that the rope matched the bruising on her wrists, so the same type of rope was used to restrain her while she was being held.

Garner digested the information and then passed the piece of paper to Brierton for her to read it and as he did, he looked up at Howton and said.

"Thanks for getting this check out so quickly."

Garner then looked around towards Brierton and said.

"So, we have Kurzwell with the threats and the drugs angle and the husband with the marital problems and the fact it was his car used to move the body."

While Garner was making this statement, Parsons was preparing to make a call to the social services office.

Twenty-Six

Parsons picked up the handset of the telephone on his desk and called the social work department. Once his call was answered, he said.

"This is Allan Parsons of Humberside Police. Can you put me through to James Bryde please?"

The person on the other end of the call responds with.

"One moment, I'll put you through to his phone."

The line went quiet while he was put through.

To Parsons' surprise, he heard a female voice on the other end of the line.

"Hi, this is Sarah. Can I help you? James is currently out of the office, and I do not know when he will be back."

Parsons replied,

"No problem. You may be able to help me out. James had printed off a list of case files showing what cases Nicki Diss was working on. Could you supply me with the same sort of list for Lesley Garth, please? And if possible, could the list include what case files Lesley also had signed out."

"Would you be able to send me a new list via email, please?"

"Sure, give me your email address and I will send it to you straight away."

Parsons gave Sarah his email address and said.

"Thanks for your help. Bye."

He then ended the call and carried on with things while he waited for the list to come through to his computer. After about five minutes, there was a loud ping on his computer to tell him a new email had arrived for him.

He looked through the email and compared it with the files he had removed from the metal filing box but things were not as expected so he called over to where Garner and Brierton were sitting, saying.

"This is strange."

"What's that," Garner replies.

"Well, I got the list of cases that Sarah had sent through from the social work office, but it shows there may be a missing file. Are you sure you got all the files that were at the house?"

Brierton looked over to Parsons and said, "Yes, all the files that we found at the house are in the box I gave you."

Garner chipped into their conversation and said, "OK, go through the files and see if you can work out what one is missing. I'll get in touch with the officers at the house and see if they can find another one there. In the meantime Becca, why don't you head down to the social services office and see if you can get some details of the missing file."

Brierton started to get ready to leave the

office and said to Parsons, "Is there a number for the file that's missing?"

"Yes, here you go," Parsons said as he wrote some details onto a small sticky notepad and handed the note to Brierton as she headed out of the office.

Twenty-Seven

Brierton had made her way out of the team's office and found herself once again in the reception area of the social work department. It was getting to the end of the working day for the office staff so she was unsure that Sarah would even still be in the office or that someone else would be able to help.

As she approached the reception desk she said, "Hi, I'm Detective Sergeant Brierton, Can I speak to Sarah, please?"

"Hang on, I think she is still here. I'll call her and ask her to come down and get you."

"Thanks."

After a few minutes, a female appeared in the reception area and walked over to where Brierton was waiting.

"Hi, I'm Sarah are you, Detective Sergeant Brierton."

"Yes, I am. I'm sorry to bother you again, but I need to speak to you about the case list you sent Allan Parsons."

"There is an extra case listed on the list, but we did not find the file at Lesley Garth's house. Would you be able to give me the details of the missing file?"

Sarah said, "OK, come up to the office and we can have a look at the case in question. I take it you have not been able to find Lesley then? It's very worrying."

As they both headed upstairs to the office area of the social workers Brierton said, "No, we have still not located her but we will continue to look for her."

Once they had got to Sarah's desk, Sarah asked, "What's the case number of the missing file?"

"7636385" Brierton replied.

"Thanks, I'll look it up on the system."

"Right, it looks like a case that involved a mother of two boys who died because of a drink and drug problem. The boys were adopted but unfortunately not together."

Brierton asked. "Is it a recent case or an old one? Is it possible to look at the file?"

To which Sarah replied, "It's an old case going back many years. The system shows the file was taken out by Lesley some time ago, but I can get some of the details printed so you can look at them."

Brierton thought for a moment and then replied, "That would be great, can you do that please?"

Sarah went back to looking at her computer screen and after a few clicks of her mouse, she stood up and walked across the office to collect some paper printouts from a printer, returned to her desk and handed the papers to Brierton.

Twenty-Eight

Lesley Garth woke up and slowly realised her hands were tied in front of her body and that she was lying on the floor. She looked around, but the room she was in was dark and seemed somewhat damp. Once she regained some more sense of consciousness, she sat up and remembered what had happened. She had been sitting in her kitchen reading when a masked person had come in through her back door and grabbed her. The last thing she remembered was feeling sleepy and passing out. She now realised the intruder must have injected her with something that knocked her out.

As she felt more and more awake, she took another look around her surroundings.

The room seemed to be empty at first,

but as Lesley's eyes adjusted to the very low light in the room, she spotted a small table near what appeared to be a door. It was this door that allowed a small amount of light in, as there was a thin gap around it.

The light coming from around the door did not appear to be sunlight, so she was sure this room was within a building of some sort.

Lesley got to her feet and made her way towards the door where she found a door handle that even though her hands were tied together, she could grip and turn the handle, but to no avail. The door opened slightly, but it was secured by what sounded like a chain on the opposite side of the door to her.

"Help, please help me."

She screamed as loud as she could but because she was still groggy from whatever had made her sleep screaming felt hard, so she turned to the table and picked up the bottle of water. She could get the cap off the bottle easily, as it had already been partially opened.

As Lesley drank from the bottle, she heard someone at the door of the room. She realised they must have heard her calling for help. She moved away from the door as she heard the chain securing the door shut being rattled and removed. Then the door opened, and someone walked into the room.

Even though the door was now open, there was still only a small amount of light in the room which meant Lesley could still see very little and because the light was coming from behind the person who had walked into the room, she could not make out any features that would give her a clue who it was.

"Why are you doing this to me?" She asked her captor as they entered the room.

"Why are you doing this?" she asked again.

Suddenly, the shadowy figure in the room said.

"Shut up. You brought all of this on yourself."

Lesley froze as although she could not see the person's face, she realised it was a male and that she knew the voice but was not fully awake so was not able to put a face to it.

"You need to feel the pain I have felt for years." He replied.

Lesley then asked, "Did you kill my Nicki?"

To which the male answered "Yes."

Lesley asked again, "But why? What have we ever done to you?"

The male moved towards Lesley and walked behind her and said.

"Your incompetence allowed me and my brother to be split up when our mother died, and then he died. If you had kept us together, I could have looked after him and he would still be alive today and so would your precious Nicki."

Lesley felt a coldness running through her as she realised who was standing in the room with her.

But before she could say anything else, her captor grabbed her arm and injected her with something. She began to feel sleepy again and then passed out.

Twenty-Nine

Brierton was reading through the papers that Sarah had given to her and suddenly saw something within the papers that surprised her. She looked up at Sarah and said.

"I need to speak to my boss about this straight away."

Brierton took her mobile out of her pocket and called Garner, who after a short while answered the call.

"Sir, the file that was not on the list we saw earlier is about two brothers being taken away from their mother because of her death."

"She was a drug addict and alcoholic. The medical reports state that led to her death."

"The brothers were put up for adoption together but were split up and went to different parts of the country."

"The thing is, one of the adopted brothers committed suicide a few years ago."

Brierton paused as Garner asked, "are there any indications as to why and how he killed himself."

"Yes, apparently, he struggled with drink and drugs like his mother. But the thing is, he killed himself by hanging himself under a pier."

Brierton paused once more and then said.

"Sarah, how can we get more information about the adoptions?"

Sarah replied, "wait here, I'll see if I can get hold of the adoption details and the file relating to the other brother." And walked away from her desk.

Brierton returned to the call with Garner and said, "Sarah is going to get some more information about the adoptions that took place. I will call you back as soon as I have something."

At this, she ended the call and placed her phone back into her pocket.

After a few minutes, Sarah returned to the office where Brierton is waiting. Brierton noticed Sarah had a shocked look about her now.

"What's wrong?" Brierton asked her.

"I've got the adoption records here and I think you need to read them."

Brierton said.

"OK, let me see them."

Sarah handed Brierton the paperwork and Brierton looked at them and very quickly started to use her phone and called Garner.

"Sir, the surviving brother's name is Bryde, James Bryde."

Garner said.

"That's the guy you spoke to at the social services office earlier, isn't it?"

"Yes." Replied Brierton.

"OK, we need to find him and bring him in for questioning. I'll put out an alert for him. Ask there if anyone knows where he might be and let the control room know."

Brierton replies. "OK Sir, I'll ask around and see what I can find out and text you everything I can find out," and ended the call.

Brierton turned to Sarah and said.

"Do you have any idea of where James Bryde may be at this time? We need to speak to him."

Sarah replied, "He may be at home as he had been calling in sick on and off a lot for the last week or so."

Brierton replied. "Can you get me his address? We will try there first."

Thirty

A police van followed by a marked police car and an ambulance had made their way up a narrow country lane and pulled up just out of sight of a small cottage set back from the road behind a hedge.

Two uniformed officers and Garner get out of the car and four uniformed officers got out of the van's side door. The officers from the van made their way along the cottage's path and headed to the rear of the property while Garner and the two officers from the car headed along the path towards the front door of the house.

As Garner approached the front door one of the officers who had made their way around to the back of the house sent out a message using his radio, "We are in position at the rear of the house, sir."

This message was the signal for the teams to start the process of getting into the house. Garner knocked on the front door and all three waited to see if anyone answered and opened the door. No reply to Garner knocking on the door was forthcoming so Garner knocked on the door once again and shouted.

"James Bryde, this is the police. Please open the door."

Once again, no response came from within the house and just as Garner was going to knock for a third and final time, a loud crashing sound is heard coming from within the house.

"Right, get this door open," Garner said, looking at the officer with him who had a large battering device with him that enabled them to break open doors if required.

The officer took a step towards the door and swung to battering device backwards and then forwards against the door. Fortunately, the door was quite old and easily flies open once struck. The officer then stood aside so the second officer and Garner could rush into the house, followed by the other uniformed officer once he had dropped the device he had used to force the door open.

Once in the house, the officers split up and make a cursory search of the downstairs rooms and Garner made his way towards the back of the building and into the kitchen.

Suddenly, a message came over on all of the officer's radios, "We've got him. He came out through the back door."

Garner took his radio from his pocket and pressed the button to speak, "OK, well done. Can two of you get him into the van and the rest of you start looking around to see if Lesley Garth is here? We can deal with the formalities with him once we have searched the building and surrounding area."

A Voice on the radio replied, "OK, will do sir. We have him cuffed so we won't be long."

Thirty-One

Once the officers taking Bryde to the van returned to the cottage, they joined the others who were milling around the house and garden looking for any signs of Lesley Garth being present.

As they searched inside the house, one of the officers called out, "Sir, there's a door here, under the stairs."

Garner moved over to the staircase area of the house and found the officer opening a door and preparing to go through it. Once he had opened the door he looked into the area behind it and said.

"There are stairs leading down to what looks like another door, I'll go down and see what's down there."

The officer made his way down to the

other door and realised there was a chain being used to keep it locked. There was no padlock on it, just a rusty type of snap hook holding the chain together to stop the door from being opened from the other side.

The officer removed the hook from the chain which then removed the chain. He could now open the door and enter the room.

"It's very dark in here, can someone pass me a torch?"

Garner turned to an officer standing behind him and said, "quickly, give me your torch."

An officer behind Garner passed him a torch that he had switched on. Garner then made his way down the stairs and passed the torch on to the officer in the basement room who used it to illuminate the room.

"She's here. She's lying on the floor." The officer shouted, "Get the ambulance guys in here."

Garner followed the officer into the room

and saw Lesley Garth lying on the basement floor, she was not moving.

Garner and the other officer who had been behind him on the stairs moved into the room and away from the door so the ambulance crew could get in and administer medical help to Lesley.

One of the ambulance technicians said, "She is responsive and is breathing fine, but she seems to have been drugged. Can we get some help to get our stretcher down here? We can then get her out of here and into the ambulance and off to the hospital, where can make a better assessment of her condition."

Garner went to the bottom of the stairs and called out to the officers waiting at the top of them, "Can you get the ambulance crews stretcher from outside the house and bring it down here, quickly."

Once the stretcher had been brought down the stairs, Lesley was placed on it and the ambulance crew took her out of the house and into the ambulance. Once she was secured in the back of the ambulance it rushed off with its lights flashing and sirens sounding followed by the police car that had brought Garner to the house.

Garner made his way out of the house and down the path and now stood at the end of the lane. He took his mobile phone out of his pocket, and selected Brierton's entry in his address book and pressed the call button.

Once the call was connected, he said.

"Hi. You probably know by now we have found Lesley Garth. She is alive and on her way to the hospital. We also have Bryde in custody and will be bringing him into the station in a while."

He paused to allow Brierton to take in what he had said and then continued.

"Can you head back to the station, and get George Diss released and taken to the hospital."

Brierton said, "Will do, what about Kurzwell?"

Garner said, "I suppose we will have to let him go for now, but we will be bringing him back in soon, I'm sure." Garner then finished by saying, "Oh and by the way. We found the missing case file and Nicki Diss's handbag here with a spare key to her husband's car, so I expect that will turn out to be how Bryde got access to the car to move Nicki's body."

About the Author

John Messingham was born in Hampton, Middlesex, England. After finishing school, he joined the British Army and served as an Infantryman and later trained as a radio operator within the battalion mortar platoon. After his time in the army, he trained as a computer programmer and started a long career in IT. The fiction he writes sometimes draws on both his military and IT backgrounds.

For more information about John and his writing, please visit:

https://johnmessingham.co.uk

By John Messingham

DCI Garner and DS Brierton Novelettes

Series One

The Pier

The Body in the Van

Murder in the Park

Short Stories

The Water Thieves

Reece Leach Short Stories One

The Watchers

Printed in Great Britain
by Amazon

24400664R00071